FISH
MY WINEGROUSE
BACK TO BLACK
LITTLE
MINKS
DNA
LUST FOR LIFE
ONEBYONE
LLAMADELREY
BORN TO DIE
ITISH SEAL POWER
PEN SE
N SANE
FLOYD
THE
GULL
KOALA MINOGUE
KOALA
(A)
KITTY PERRY
DADDY
REVER
oose
ingsteen
rkness
the Edge
Town
CLUCK
BERRY
JUSTIN BEAVER
ndy Wartho

EWE2 OCTOBER
DE LA SWAN
AND RISING
GULLS ALOUD
nine Inch Snails
TAKE RAT & PARTY
Salmon and Garfunkel
Bridge Over Troubled
MOUSE ORIGIN OF SYMMETRY
the bends
MICE GIRLS
MANIC STREET POOCHES
EVERYTHING MUST GO
Alpaca
Morrissette

BAND TOGETHER

written and illustrated by Chloe Douglass

Magination Press • Washington, DC • American Psychological Association

Duck lived by himself.

Most days Duck fished, ate lunch,

combed the beach, made tea by himself …

... Duck was a solo act.

Duck was so used to
being by himself,

he found making friends
a little bit overwhelming.

Heading home one afternoon, Duck heard a call.

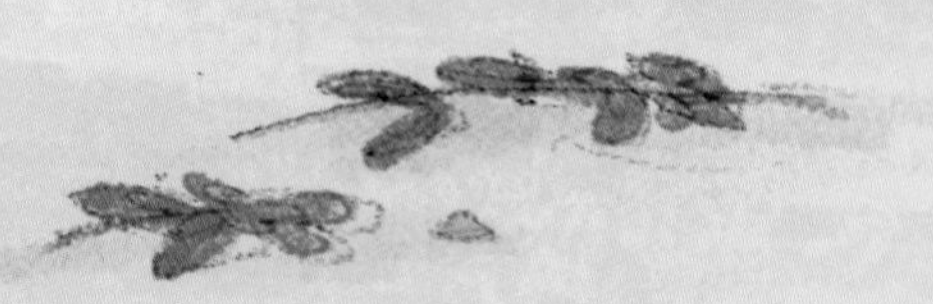

"Hi! Can you lend a wing?"
Duck wanted to shy away but ...

Duck couldn't think of a reason quickly enough to say no.
And before he knew what he was doing,
Duck was joining in celebrating the van being fixed!

“Thanks so much,” said Fox.
“We’re playing a concert tomorrow,” said Bear.
“It’d be great to see you again,” said Seagull.

Duck waddled home and thought
how much fun that had been.

Maybe he could ask the band if they would want to play with him again?

But before long the same old doubt came creeping in …

Why would Bear, Fox, and Seagull want to be friends with a duck like him?

The day of the concert arrived!
Not all was going as planned.

“Could you stand in for Seagull this evening? We can’t go on without another player!”

Duck knew deep down he should take a chance, but he shook his head sadly.

“I hope you change
your mind,” Bear sighed.

ENRIQUE
CONCERT TONIGHT!!

CONCERT
TONIGHT!

Bear and Fox were about to cancel the show when …

... a great quacking
came through the crowd!

“What’s this!?” Bear grinned.
“Here to help my friends a little,” Duck said.

They played long into the night …

… and the solo act joined The Band and hit the road with his new friends.

THE BAND

Chloe Douglass works in her home studio to create illustrations, character designs, and story ideas. She graduated from Kingston University with an MA Illustration degree in 2012. She lives in Tooting, London. Visit chloeillustrates.co.uk or visit her on Twitter @chloillustrates and Instagram @chloeillustrates.

Magination Press is the children's book imprint of the American Psychological Association. Through APA's publications, the association shares with the world mental health expertise and psychological knowledge. Magination Press books reach young readers and their parents and caregivers to make navigating life's challenges a little easier. It's the combined power of psychology and literature that makes a Magination Press book special. Visit www.maginationpress.org.

Magination Press is a registered trademark of the American Psychological Association. Order books at maginationpress.org, or call 1-800-374-2721.

Book design by Gwen Grafft

Printed by Phoenix Color, Hagerstown, MD

Library of Congress Cataloging-in-Publication Data

Names: Douglass, Chloe, author.
Title: Band Together / by Chloe Douglass.
Description: Washington, DC : Magination Press, an imprint of American Psychological Association, 2020. | Summary: Duck spends so much time alone that making new friends seem overwhelming, but when a rowdy band needs his help he finds it hard to say no.
Identifiers: LCCN 2019049183 | ISBN 9781433832413 (hardcover)
Subjects: CYAC: Friendship—Fiction. | Anxiety—Fiction. | Bands (Music)—Fiction. | Ducks—Fiction. | Animals—Fiction.
Classification: LCC PZ7.1.D6815 Wit 2020 | DDC [E]—dc23
LC record available at https://lccn.loc.gov/2019049183

Manufactured in the United States of America
10 9 8 7 6 5 4 3 2 1

For Pedro, and everyone else along the way that always believed in Bear, Duck, and their friends — *CD*

Lust For Life
LITTLE MINKS
DNA
ONEBYONE
WINEGROUSE
BACK TO BLACK
LLAMA DEL REY
SEAL POWER
BORN TO DIE
SANE
FLOYD THE GULL
KOALA MINOGUE
KOALA
(A)
KITTY PERRY
DADDY
Town
CLUCK BERRY
JUSTIN BEAVER

DE LA SWAN
AND RISING
GULLS ALOUD
TAKE RAT & PARTY
nine Inch Snails
Salmon and Garfunkel
Bridge Over Troubled
MOUSE ORIGIN OF SYMMETRY
the bends
MICE GIRLS
MANIC STREET POOCHES
EVERYTHING MUST GO
Alpaca
Morrissette